NANCY DREW

HOLLYWOOD
Head Scratchers

By Jen Funk Weber

New York   London   Toronto   Sydney

An imprint of Simon & Schuster Children's Publishing Division
1230 Avenue of the Americas, New York, NY 10020

Manufactured in the United States of America
First Edition
2 4 6 8 10 9 7 5 3 1
ISBN-13: 978-1-4169-3380-9
ISBN-10: 1-4169-3380-8

To solve her cases, Nancy notes which facts are common to every witness's story and which are not.

There are twenty symbols in each box, but only five of the symbols appear in all four boxes. Which five symbols do the boxes have in common?

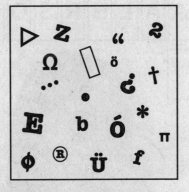

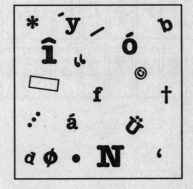

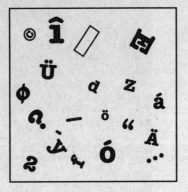

Nancy recommends an improvement be made in the school cafeteria. What is it?

*To find out, read the letters above the numbers in order from 1 to 8. As it appears below, **A, Z, F, P** are the letters above 1, 2, 3, 4. Since this is not the beginning of any word, mentally slide the number string to the right until you find Nancy's suggested improvement by reading the letters in order from 1 to 8.*

I	P	A	Z	F	D	A	A	A	L	B	R	S	O	G
5	4	7	2	3	6	8	1							

Answer:

____ ____ ____ ____ ____

____ ____ ____

NANCY'S CALLING

Nancy has dialed in to a number of goals that she wants to achieve during her stay in Hollywood. Crack this code to name one.

Each number stands for one of the letters found with it on the telephone. You determine which one. A number may represent a different letter each time it's used. For instance, in **N-A-N-C-Y** *(6 2 6 2 9), 2 represents A the first time it's used and C the next.*

	ABC	DEF
1	**2**	**3**
GHI	**JKL**	**MNO**
4	**5**	**6**
PRS	**TUV**	**WXY**
7	**8**	**9**
*	**QZ**	**#**
	0	

One of Nancy's goals in Hollywood:

86   23   2   667625   83362437

___ ___   ___ ___   ___

___ ___ ___ ___ ___ ___

___ ___ ___ ___ ___ ___ ___ ___

5

CORKY SAYS

Pretend Corky is Simon and do what Corky says—and only what Corky says. If you're successful, you'll discover . . . well . . . something that Corky says!

	1	2	3	4	5	6
A	Because	True	I	Though	Think	When
B	The	Smart	Question	Ability	Heart	To
C	Detective	Sleuth	Best	Common	Is	Many
D	An	Sense	Cannot	Attractive	Care	Believe
E	Follow	It	Quality	Lesson	Answer	Of
F	In	Few	A	Impart	Woman	Art

1. Corky says, "Cross off every word that rhymes with 'Drew' in column 2."
2. Corky says, "Cross off all the words in columns 1 and 6 with more than three letters."
3. Corky says, "Cross off every word in column 4 and row D that does not start with a vowel."
4. Corky says, "Cross off all the words in rows F and B that rhyme with 'start.'"
5. Corky says, "Cross off every word with an even number of letters in column 3 and row E."
6. Corky says, "Read the remaining words to read the best line in the whole movie."

Answer: _____ _____ _____ _____ _____ _____

_____ _____ _____ _____ _____ _____ .

Ned, Nancy, and Corky form a sort of triangle.

How many triangles can you find in the image below? Don't be hasty—triangles can be any size. We've found the first one.

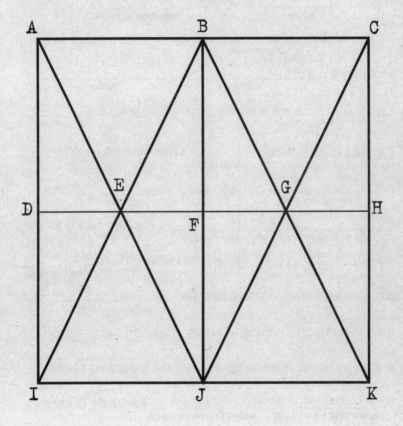

Triangles
1- ADE

Ask your friends to provide words to fill the holes in this story.

A good _____ is always _____, and
      noun   *verb ending in "ed"*

having certain _____ on hand always helps. I
               plural noun

recommend a _____ _____ .
                adjective   *noun*

I _____ mine all the time. In it I keep a _____ .
     verb   *noun*

Be sure to check the _____ now and then so you're
                     plural noun

not _____ . I also keep a _____ for
     past tense verb   *noun*

_____ _____ . It's also handy to keep
verb ending in "ing"   *plural noun*

some _____ for those times when you're _____
        food   *verb ending
                                                          in "ing"*

and can't get away, or to share with _____ . But
                                     person's name

the most important thing to always have on hand, the one

thing you never want to be without, the thing that every

_____ _____ keeps by his/her
repeat first verb used   *repeat first noun used*

side is a _____ .
            noun

BOOKMARK

If you read as much as Nancy Drew, you can probably use a bookmark or two.

Materials
- ¼ yard (9 inches) ribbon
- Needle and matching thread
- Fabric glue (optional)
- Beads, tassels, and charms of your choice

1. Place ribbon wrong side up on table. **Figure 1.**

2. Fold **B** to **C** so bottom cut edge meets right ribbon edge, forming point at D. **Figure 2.**

3. Fold **D** to **A**, forming point in center of ribbon. **Figure 3**.

4. Stitch or glue in place.

5. Repeat steps 2–4 at top.

6. Stitch bead, charm, or tassel at top, leaving bottom point plain so it can be closed into a book.

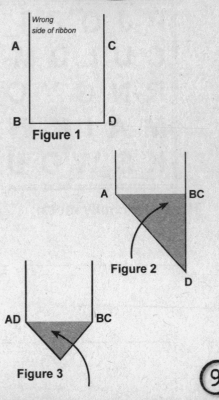

Cross off every letter that appears three times (and only three times). Write the remaining letters in order, from top to bottom and left to right, to spell the Drew family motto.

P	J	O	P	T	G	H	U	N	L
C	U	L	D	M	W	K	A	G	E
R	N	G	Y	C	N	S	F	D	J
M	A	I	K	W	J	Y	L	Y	R
K	S	W	D	U	A	M	T	P	C

The Drew family motto:

____ ____ ____ ____ ____

____ ____ ____ ____

Nancy Drew has done it again. She and all her friends are mixed up in crime. Can you sort things out for them?

Each group of letters contains the name of one of Nancy's friends and a crime. Each is spelled correctly, but the two are mixed up together. Can you separate the friends from the crimes?

> ***Example:*** CONYSPOIRUACY
> ***Friend:*** YOU ***Crime:*** CONSPIRACY

BARSOENSS

___ ___ ___ ___ : ___ ___ ___ ___ ___

BRINBEREDY

___ ___ ___ : ___ ___ ___ ___ ___ ___ ___

TEXRTORITISONH

___ ___ ___ ___ ___ : ___ ___ ___ ___ ___ ___ ___

KCIDNOARPPKINYG

___ ___ ___ ___ ___ : ___ ___ ___ ___ ___ ___ ___ ___ ___ ___

GFOERORGERGEY

___ ___ ___ ___ ___ ___ : ___ ___ ___ ___ ___ ___ ___

SITANLKGIANG

___ ___ ___ ___ : ___ ___ ___ ___ ___ ___ ___ ___

And, by the way, what's the name of this puzzle?

_____

A THOROUGH SEARCH

Nancy searches every corner for clues. Will you help? You search this house while Nancy searches next door. The homeowners might come home anytime, so be quick about it. (Don't forget: You must pass through every white square only once!)

START

STOP

Throw a Nancy Drew party!

To invite your friends, fill out the invitation below. Take it to a copy shop and reduce it until the text requires a magnifying glass to read. (You can also type the invitation on a computer using Times New Roman at a 4-point setting and print it yourself.) Place the miniature invitation in an envelope with a magnifying glass and hand-deliver it to your guests. Inexpensive magnifying glasses can be found in party supply stores.

Dear _____,

You are cordially invited to attend a
Nancy Drew Mystery Party.

Time: _____

Date: _____

Place: _____

Appropriate dress, please. I hope you attend.

RSVP: _____   _____

Signature

Make **Flower Table Treats** and **Nancy-Fancy Napkins** for your party. Serve **Secret Message Popcorn Balls** and **Hot Cocoa**. Have a **Taffy Pull** and a **Scavenger Hunt**. Play **Detective** and complete a **Hole Story**.

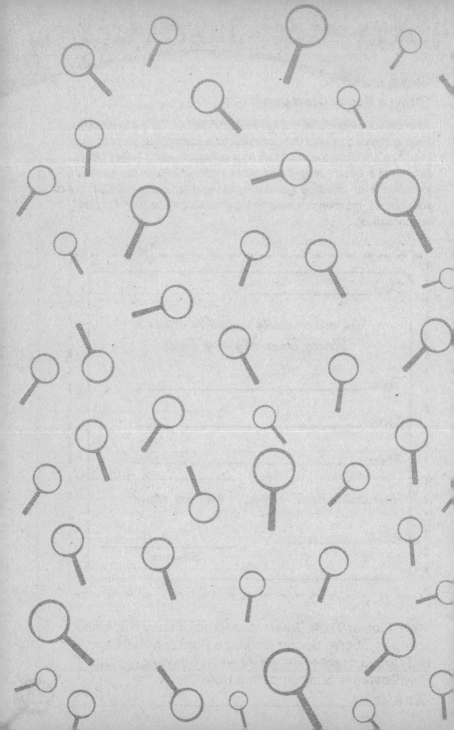

MYSTERIOUS CONNECTIONS

Nancy Drew is determined to find out what Dashiel Biedermeyer is hiding.

Follow the clues below carefully to uncover a mysterious connection.

1. *Print the name BIEDERMEYER.*

   1. _____

2. *Copy the last letter as you read from the left to the first position.*

   2. _____

3. *Delete the letter that comes last in the alphabet.*

   3. _____

4. *Move the second consonant from the right to the second position from the left.*

   4. _____

   5. _____

5. *Delete the fourth vowel from the right.*

6. *Make every vowel that appears only once a U.*

   6. _____

7. *Switch the second and fourth letters from the left.*

   7. _____

8. *Delete the third letter from the left.*

   8. _____

9. *Delete the first vowel from the right.*

   9. _____

10. *Reverse the first three letters from the left.*

    10. _____

Answer: _____

CAUGHT RED-HANDED

How many of these "red" words can you identify? If you get caught on the tough ones, will you see red, or will your face turn red? Nancy did the first one to get you started. Red-dy?

How most people feel after midnight	**T I R E D**
Extra ____ might boost your grade in school	**___ R E D ___ ___**
Have nowhere to go, nothing to do, and no one to do it with	**___ ___ R E D**
Stone age dad	**___ R E D**
Tell the future	**___ R E D ___ ___ ___**
Rip paper to bits	**___ ___ R E D**
Tallest tree on earth	**R E D ___ ___ ___ ___**
Hunter	**___ R E D ___ ___ ___ ___**

Use the Morse code key to decipher a quote from the Nancy Drew movie.

•— **A**	—••• **B**	—•—• **C**	—•• **D**	• **E**	••—• **F**
——• **G**	•••• **H**	•• **I**	•——— **J**	—•— **K**	•—•• **L**
—— **M**	—• **N**	——— **O**	•——• **P**	——•— **Q**	•—• **R**
••• **S**	— **T**	••— **U**	•••— **V**	•—— **W**	—••— **X**
—•—— **Y**	——•• **Z**				

•• ——— — / • —— ——— ••— / — •••• •• • •— — /

— — — — — — — — — — —

—— •—— / —— •• — •• / ••• ••• / •— /

— — — — — — — — — — —

•—• ——— •—— •••• ••—•— ••— •—•• /

— — — — — — — —

— •—— ——— •—••

— — — —?

Who said it? _____

Where do spies sleep?

Decode the answer by filling in the blanks to complete the sequence. It's as easy as ABC! (Hint: One is done for you.)

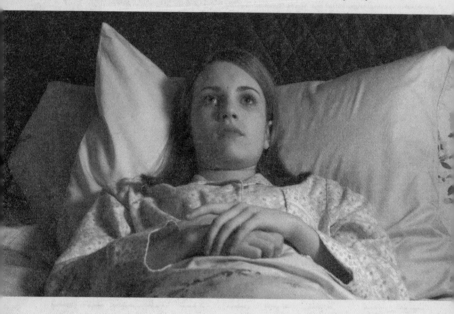

R		A		O		L		B		P
S		B		P		M		C		Q
T		C		Q		N		D		R

R

___ ___ ___ ___ **R** ___ ___ ___ ___ ___

		O		F		D		W		S
		P		G		E		X		T
		Q		H		F		Y		U

PUZZLE PIECES

Nancy's never sure until the end how the pieces of a puzzle fit together.

Find and shade these four puzzle pieces in the picture below.

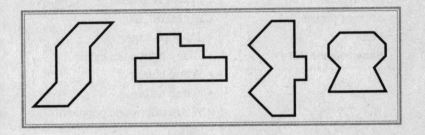

SECRET MESSAGE POPCORN BALLS

Hide secret messages for your friends in these chewy, sweet popcorn balls!

Materials for messages
- Slips of paper
- Pens
- Easy-release foil

Popcorn Ball ingredients
- 1¼ cups sugar
- ¼ cup light corn syrup
- ½ cup butter
- ⅓ cup water
- ½ cup unpopped popcorn
- Salt
- Candy thermometer

1. Write messages on slips of paper. (See page 21 for ideas.)

2. Cut foil about 4 inches square. Fold foil over secret messages, being sure easy release side is on the outside. Roll into a small cylinder and set aside.

3. Pop popcorn. Pour into large bowl. Salt. Set aside.

4. Mix sugar, corn syrup, butter, and water in saucepan. Cook over medium heat until syrup reaches 300 degrees Farenheit on a candy thermometer.

5. Pour mixture over popcorn and mix well so that popcorn is coated evenly.

6. When candied popcorn is cool enough to handle, work quickly with buttered hands to form a baseball-size ball of popcorn around each message. Set aside. When cool, wrap in plastic, foil, or waxed paper.

Makes 10–12 balls.

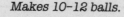

Popcorn Sur-Prize

Insert messages that say "Thanks for eating!" in all but one popcorn ball. In the last ball, insert a message that says, "Winner!" Offer a prize for the winner.

Popcorn Puzzle

Draw a map or write a message telling players where to find a surprise, or the next game. Cut the map/message into 10 pieces (funny shapes are good). Insert one piece into each popcorn ball. After players eat the snacks, they must put the pieces together to discover where to go next.

Pop Fortunes

Cut apart the fortunes below—or make up your own—and insert one into each ball.

When the wind blows, your ears whistle "Pachelbel's Canon."	You would do well to learn the words to "Row, Row, Row Your Boat" backward.
Your elbow hums when you bend it, but only cats can hear it.	Congratulations! Someone just named a camel after you.
Your feet smell like roses: the ones from three years ago.	You nose hairs will grow really, really long so you can braid them.
Your lucky color is puce. But it becomes unlucky if you wear it with red, blue, green, yellow, purple, brown, black, or white.	You hold the key to the mystery of the deadly celery stick skateboard doll.
Don't get on a boat with three girls wearing orange vests unless you have cinnamon gum.	The brother of the leader of the Azignorks from Igglebah 9 looks exactly like you!
People find you irresistible when you eat spinach with vinegar and pine nuts.	You will misplace your keys someday.

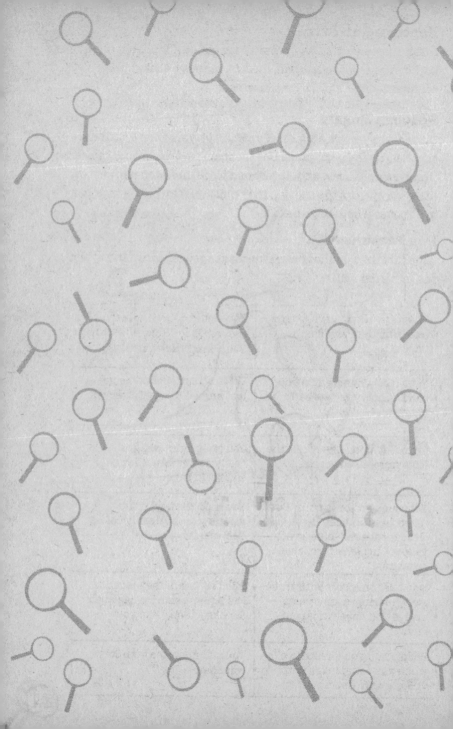

We asked Nancy, "What do you do when there's a kidnapping?"

To read her answer, start with a letter in one of the corners (no, we're not telling you which one), then read every third letter, clockwise around the square, until all letters are used.

H Q N I U T

O   M

E   I

E   W

D   U

B K T P A E

Answer:

___ ___ ___ ___ ___ ___ ___

,

___ ___ ___ ___ ___ ___ ___

___ ___ ___ ___ ___ .

GET A CLUE

In fact, get a bunch of clues, sort them out, and piece them together!

Place the words below into the grid so they crisscross like a crossword. We've done one to get you started.

3	**4**	**5**	**6**	**7**	**8**	**9**
CUE	HINT	GOODS	BODING	INKLING	~~EVIDENCE~~	INTUITION
KEY	LEAD	HUNCH	NOTION	POINTER		SUSPICION
TIP	SIGN	SENSE		WITNESS		
	WIND	TRACE				
		TRAIL				

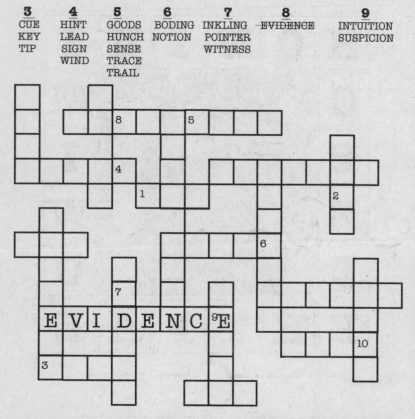

Write the letters in the numbered boxes on the spaces with the same numbers to reveal the result of your work.

___ ___ ___ ___   ___ ___ ___ ___ ___ ___
1 **2** **3** **4**   **5** **6** **7** **8** **9** **10**

JAIL TIME

**Whew! It's been a busy summer!
Nancy has helped put eight outlaws behind bars.**

*Each criminal is doing time for 1 to 8 years. No two crooks are
in jail for the same amount of time. The number in each circle is
the total years in jail for all the offenders whose sections meet at
that circle. For instance, 25 is the total number of years Sydonia,
Cassie, Wayne, and CJ will spend in jail. How many years did each
outlaw get?*

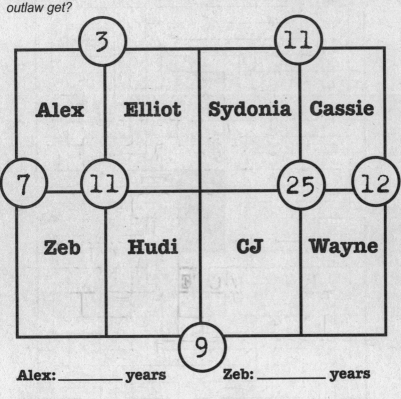

Alex: _____ years

Elliot: _____ years

Sydonia: _____ years

Cassie: _____ years

Zeb: _____ years

Hudi: _____ years

CJ: _____ years

Wayne: _____ years

ESCAPE!

Nancy has been kidnapped and locked in a room in an old theater. How will she escape—by the door, a window, a vent, or a secret tunnel?

Exit

Vent

Window

Exit

Tunnel

Exit

Exit

Exit

A NANCY-FANCY NAPKIN

Nancy Drew appreciates an elegant touch. A simply folded napkin creates an air of fine dining—even in the school cafeteria!

1. Unfold a square dinner napkin—paper or cloth—and lay it on a table so a corner points to you. It will look like a diamond.

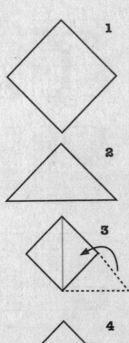

2. Fold the bottom corner to the top, to make a triangle.

3. Fold the left and right corners to the top, to make a small diamond.

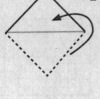

4. Fold the bottom corner to the top, to make a small triangle.

5. Bring the bottom corners of the triangle toward each other, and tuck one corner into the fold of the other.

6. Shape the base into a circle so the napkin can stand, points up, on a plate. Or flatten the circle to stow-and-go in a lunch box.

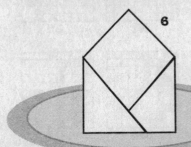

CON ARTIST

Use a sharp pencil to copy the puzzle pieces below into the correct squares on the grid to create a picture. The correct square is the one where the letter and number below each piece intersect.

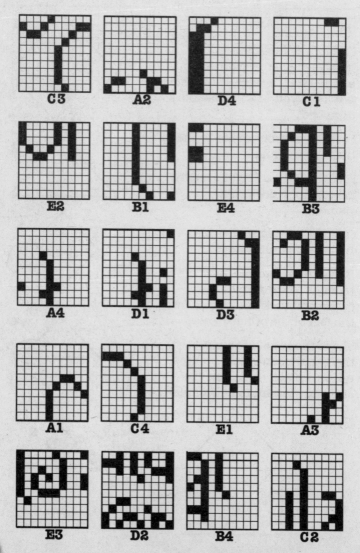

C3 A2 D4 C1

E2 B1 E4 B3

A4 D1 D3 B2

A1 C4 E1 A3

E3 D2 B4 C2

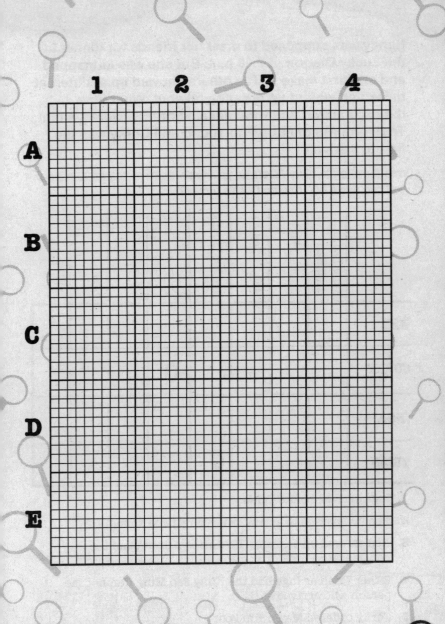

DINNER DISASTER

Nancy was supposed to meet her friends for dinner at the Lucky Dragon at 7:00 p.m. But she was kidnapped and couldn't make it. The others showed up at different times and wound up ordering takeout. What time did each arrive, and what did s/he order? (Here's a hint: Trish ordered the Egg Foo Young and Corky was the first to arrrive.)

Use the chart to record facts as you discover them. Put an X in a box if you can rule it out. Use an O if it's a match.

	Kung Pao Ming Har	Mu Shoo Pork	Mao Po Tou Foo	Egg Foo Young	6:30	6:45	7:00	7:30
NED								
CORKY					O			
INGA								
TRISH				O				

1. Inga arrived before Trish.

2. The last person to arrive ordered Egg Foo Young.

3. Ned showed up on time. (He's always prompt and considerate.)

4. Either Trish or Inga had the Kung Pao Ming Har, not the person who arrived at 6:30.

5. Corky ordered Ma Po Tou Foo.

30

LESSONS FROM NANCY

When Biedermeyer first meets Nancy, he asks her to teach his grandchildren something. What is it?

*To find out, read the letters above the numbers in order from 1 to 7. As it appears below, **S, L, N,** and **O** are the letters above 1, 2, 3, and 4. Since this is not the beginning of any word, mentally slide the number string to the right until you find what Nancy can teach by reading the letters in order from 1 to 7.*

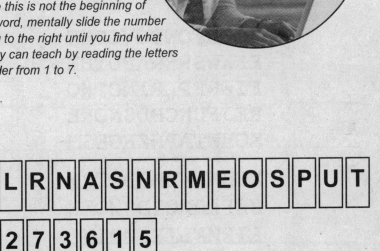

O	L	R	N	A	S	N	R	M	E	O	S	P	U	T

4	2	7	3	6	1	5

Answer:

____ ____ ____ ____ ____ ____ ____ ____

THE MIRROR'S MESSAGE

Black out the letters on the top half of the grid that have incorrect mirror images in the bottom half. The remaining letters reveal a funny movie quote. Do you know who said it?

Example: B=B

BOHHFONEGYCSHE
EKXWSREWAPDTHE
FIENEPLRINOTNO
REJFUNCHDSNOKE
XCHWTAPNZRGESM

Whose line is this? _____

THE HOLE STORY 2

Ask your friends to provide words to fill the holes in this story.

It was the _____ _____ in my career as
             adjective   *noun*

an amateur_____ . I got a_____from my
         profession   *noun*

neighbor, _____, telling me his/her _____
        person's name   *vegetables*

were being _____. I agree it was_____
      verb ending in "ed"   *adjective*

and a _____ , but it wasn't exactly the sort
       noun

_____ I was looking for. Know what I mean?
  repeat first noun

But business was slow, so I said I'd _____into it.
                          verb

The more I _____, the more it seemed like an
     same verb with "ed"

_____job. But the _____weren't adding
  adjective   *plural noun*

up, so I set up a _____. It was_____ .
             noun   *person's name*

S/he wanted to see if_____ could _____.
              repeat vegetables   *verb*

HOT COCOA SECRETS

Nancy loves hot cocoa and has been known to take a thermos to school so she can enjoy it during lunch. Here are three of her favorite cocoa-additions for when she wants a little something special. Each recipe starts with ¾ cup of hot cocoa—your favorite.

MM–MM–MINT
Add 1/8 teaspoon mint extract; stir. Top with marshmallows drizzled with chocolate syrup.

ORANGE BLISS
Add 1/8 teaspoon orange extract and 1/8 teaspoon ground cardamom; stir. Top with whipped cream sprinkled with cocoa powder.

ALLLLLMMMOND MEDITATION
Add 1/8 teaspoon almond extract; stir. Top with whipped cream sprinkled with cinnamon.

AROUND-THE-HOUSE SCAVENGER HUNT

Every item on this list is worth a certain number of points. Each person or team gathers as many items as s/he can in the allotted time. When the time is up, total the points, and crown a winner!

Item	Points
1984 penny	10
Any ball, the size of a golf ball or smaller	10
Article of clothing with the number **10** on it	20
Banana peel	10
Band-Aid	7
Barrette	5
Battery	5
Bookmark	5
Book with "of" in the title	10
Blue envelope	10
Calculator	5
Calendar	5
Candle	5
Candy wrapper	8
Can of spray paint	5
Cotton ball	5
Crayon	5
Crochet hook	10
Dead insect	20
Deck of cards	5
Dental floss	5
Dried bean	10
Drink mix	4
Dust bunny	2
Eraser	5
Flashlight	5
Fitness object	25
Food seasoning that begins with **C**	10
Frozen pea	10
Glove	5
Green bottle	5
Green jigsaw puzzle piece	20
Holiday decoration	5
Jingle bell	10

Item	Points
Key ring	5
Longest hair (everyone can get one—only the longest earns points)	10
Longest shoelace	10
Loofah	4
Magnet	5
Map	10
Measuring device, not a ruler	5
Movie with "life" in the title	10
Mug with words on it	5
Nancy Drew book	5
Orange pen	10
Paintbrush	5
Pair of dice	10
Paper clip	5
Phone number of a nearby pizza shop	5
Photograph with 3 people	20
Pink underwear	10
Pin with words on it	10
Plastic container	5
Plastic toy animal	10
Plastic toy person	10
Play money	10
Popcorn kernel	10
Postage stamp	5
Postcard	5
Post-it note	5
Purple sock	20
Red pencil	5
Ruler	5
Safety pin	5
Screwdriver	5
Sewing tool	10
Signature of the oldest person	

Item	Points
Something associated with fish	20
Something black and white	10
Something blue	5
Something checked	10
Something fuzzy	10
Something heart-shaped	10
Something musical	5
Something that begins with the letter **K**	10
Something that boys use, but girls don't	10
Something that curls	10
Something that girls use, but boys don't	10
Something that is glued	5
Something that rolls	10
Something that snaps	10
Something that squeaks	5
Something with a bird on it	7
Something with a hook	10
Something with a red lid	10
Something with dots	10
Something with holes in it	6
Something with the name of your hometown	10
Something with Velcro	10
Stick of gum	6
String	3
Striped hand towel	10
The letter **A**	20
Tomato soup can	5
Toothpick	5
Toothpaste	5
Traced outline of the longest foot in the house	10
Umbrella	5
Wire	5
Yellow sheet of paper	7

Total Points: _____

DETECTIVE

Two or more players

In this game, one player or group is the mastermind while the other is the detective. The detective has one minute to observe the scene created by the mastermind before being sent from the room. The mastermind then alters the scene in four visible ways. Alterations might include moving an object, changing a hairstyle, or untucking a shirt. The detective is called back and must guess what alterations have been made, earning a point for every correct guess. Three wrong guesses ends the turn. The detective and mastermind change roles. The player or team with the most points at the end of the game wins.

CODED QUOTE 2

*Use the code key to decipher a quote from the Nancy Drew movie. The letters for **NANCY** are provided. Can you figure out the rest?*

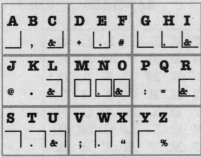

A B C	D E F	G H I
J K L	M N O	P Q R
S T U	V W X	Y Z

EXAMPLE:

N A N C Y

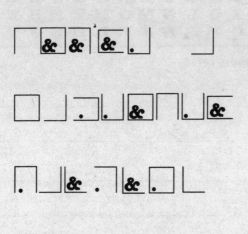

FASHION FRENZY

At home, it's Bess complaining about Nancy's fashion sense. Here, it's Inga. Help Nancy find some clothes, will you? Please?

Find and circle these clothes in the letters below. They can be found forward, backward, up, down, or diagonal. When you've found the clothes, write the unused letters in order, from top to bottom and left to right, to read Inga's thoughts on Nancy's fashion sense.

BERMUDAS   **CARGOS**   **JEANS**   **TANK**
CAMI   **FLIP FLOPS**   **MINISKIRT**   **TEE**
CARDIGAN   **HOODIE**   **SANDALS**   **VEST**

```
T W V E S T E S I L L W
R A E H M O A A Y M S B
I E N O O N G N T P A H
K E B K D O R R O I D C
S N K A O F D L A A U P
I E L N N Y F I L C M O
N S A F E P R F E T R A
I N A G I D R A C S E H
M I O L N M O M E N B E
T O F R N J E A N S O T
```

Unused letters:

__ __ __ __ ,   __ __   __ __ __   __ __

__ __   __ __ __   __ __ __ __   __ __

__   __ __ __ __ __   __ __ __ __ __

__ __ __ __ __ __ __   __ __ __ __ __ __ .

__ __   __ __ __ .

DID THEY, OR DIDN'T THEY?

When yesterday was tomorrow, Nancy Drew promised Corky, "I'll have dinner with you the day after tomorrow if my library books arrive and I can finish my research tomorrow." The library books arrived the day before yesterday, and Nancy completed her research within 24 hours.

Did Corky have dinner with Nancy?

YES or NO

IN THE LINE OF DUTY

The boxes connected by the lines contain the same letter. Some letters are given, while others have to be guessed. When you fill in all the boxes, you'll be able to read a joke that Nancy likes to tell.

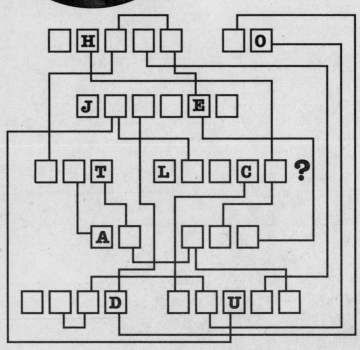

Joke: _____

_____

DIALOGUE BOXES

Decipher this bit of movie dialogue by fitting the right boxes into the empty spaces. Black squares are spaces between words, and words wrap from one line to the next.

Boxes:

- Top row: (■/B, ■/M), (L/■, M/A), (W/A, N/E), (D/■, R/L), (I/T, U/T)
- Bottom row: (■/Y, A/L), (L/S, P/■), (W/A, S/T), (R/■, I/T), (E/■, A/T)

Grid:

I			N	T		T	O			E		H	O
N	E				W			H			Y		F	A
T	H	E	R		B				I		A			O
			N	T		T	O		H	E	L			J
A				A	N			H	E			L	I	T
T	L			G	I			.				'	S	
W	H				O	U		C	A	L			A	
	M	O	R			D	I	L	E	M			.	

FLOWER TABLE TREATS

Materials
- 1 or 2 artificial leaves
- Tape
- Plastic stemmed glass
- Paper napkin
- A handful of small candies or other treats

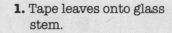

1. Tape leaves onto glass stem.

2. Unfold napkin and scrunch into glass so corners stick up, like flower petals.

3. Nestle treats inside napkin.

Nancy would like the principal of her new high school to address some important issues. One is written below. What is it?

(Hint: It helps to hold the page at eye level and shut one eye.)

LOOKING FOR LOOT

Five thieves have stashed their loot. Help Nancy Drew find it before the thieves return.

Follow the vertical lines downward until you reach a horizontal line. Travel along the horizontal line until you reach another vertical line, then take that vertical line downward again. You must take the new path at every intersection, always traveling down, left, or right. If you follow the paths correctly, you'll discover where the loot is hidden.

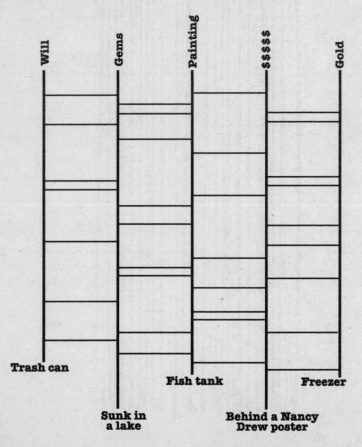

JAIL BREAK

Four synonyms of "jail" are locked up in the letter strings below. Break them out through the word windows.

Each letter string below has two panels of windows above it. Only one panel will break out a word that means "jail." In your mind, place a panel of windows over the letter string. The black squares cover unused letters while the open windows reveal the word. Write the letter of the correct panel for each letter string on a space at the bottom. Unscramble the four letters to spell another synonym of "jail."

P ▨ ▨ ▨ □ ▨ □ ▨ ▨ ▨   ▨ ▨ □ ▨ □ ▨ ▨ □ ▨ B

H P A O L K L E O Y

O ▨ ▨ □ ▨ ▨ □ ▨ □   ▨ ▨ □ ▨ ▨ ▨ □ ▨ A

A C E O M O L E W R

R □ ▨ ▨ □ ▨ □ ▨ ▨   ▨ ▨ ▨ □ □ ▨ ▨ □ C

S L A T A M M N E K

O ▨ □ ▨ □ ▨ ▨ □ ▨   □ ▨ □ ▨ ▨ □ ▨ ▨ S

R A C E L I N E K

ANSWER:

_____ _____ _____ _____

MOVIE PALS

Match the four pairs of movie pals below by drawing a line between the two. Lines can only pass through empty squares, horizontally and vertically (not diagonally), in such a way that none cross.

EXAMPLE:

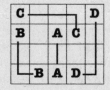

Nancy & Ned
Inga & Trish

George & Bess
Dehlia & Leshing

	Inga	Nancy			
				George	
		Trish		Dehlia	
	Bess			Ned	Leshing

SUM SHOE GUMSHOE

The four different shoes in the grid below belong to Nancy, Bess, George, and Inga. The sums of the shoe sizes are given at the end of the rows and columns. What size is each shoe?

A: George   B: Nancy   C: Bess   D.Inga

B	B	A	D	31
A	D	A	D	34
A	C	A	D	32
D	C	A	B	30
33	27	36	31	

A= _____

B= _____

C= _____

D= _____

CROOKED

An evil person is "crooked." The words in this puzzle are "crooked." Does that make this puzzle evil?

Find these 18 synonyms of "crooked" in the letters below. Watch out! Each one is crooked!

```
C U U R R O C F S B N U D L
I P N S I N A L Y T C O U U
T B L M P R E C N T U A J F
G N I L A E D E L B F N X T
B R Y I U T L B P K D A U I
C Q U N L U U L I N O R E R
F R A U D O P S A V U C D F
L A U N D E R H X S E K R S
H W J S Z I S G U D M A U U
Y M F C S K U C L O U O E B
T O L R R D O R D N D R I W
F V D U H X N A M E U E F D
I E T V P T I U F F K H E T
O H I J E U A T F A R C I W
L O S U H R L W Z R E A O S
E D W U C L N O I I J E R R
S S E A I E E O U A H R E D
S L E V I O U S H S C T N Y
U R U O R S L C R I M I D E
T E M F W A L N U S H A A X
```

CORRUPT	EVIL	TREACHEROUS
CRAFTY	FRAUDULENT	UNDERHAND
CRIMINAL	~~NEFARIOUS~~	UNLAWFUL
DECEITFUL	RUTHLESS	UNSCRUPULOUS
DEVIOUS	SHADY	VILLAINOUS
DOUBLE-DEALING	SHIFTY	WICKED

TASTY + LAUGHS = TAFFY

Nancy didn't get to have a taffy pull at her party, but you can have one!

Before machines were made to pull taffy, friends and relatives got together to share some laughs and pull a batch of taffy. Taffy starts as a thick cooked syrup. When it is cool enough to handle, it is pulled. Pulling taffy incorporates air into the syrup, transforming it into a thick, chewy, tasty candy.

WARNING:
Freshly cooked taffy syrup is extremely hot and can burn. Use caution and adult supervision with this activity.

1. Cover baking sheet with easy-release foil (easy-release side up).

2. Combine all but vanilla in a saucepan.

3. Cook on medium heat until mixture reaches the "soft crack stage" (300°F).

4. Remove from heat. Stir in vanilla. Pour onto foil-covered sheet.

5. When taffy is cool enough to handle, pick up with buttered fingers, pull, fold it back on itself, and repeat. Continue until taffy is blond, satiny, and hard to pull.

6. Form taffy into a rope, cut into 1-inch pieces, and wrap in waxed paper.

Ingredients

- 3 cups sugar
- 1/2 cup white vinegar
- 1 cup water
- 2 tablespoons butter
- 1/8 teaspoon cream of tartar
- Pinch of salt
- 1 teaspoon vanilla
- Butter for hands
- Easy-release foil
- Baking sheet
- Candy thermometer

WHODUNNIT?

Nancy lost sight of a robber as he disappeared off a busy street into a bar, restaurant, or shop. She questioned four possible witnesses:

Homeless man: "He ran into the restaurant."

Restaurant owner: "I saw him go into the bar."

Bartender: "The restaurant guy is lying; he didn't come in here."

Shopkeeper: "I don't know where he went, but he didn't come in here."

Three of the four witnesses are telling the truth; one is lying. Nancy now knows where to look for the robber, and who might be an accomplice. Do you?

STRING OF CLUES

Somebody tracked mud all through the kitchen and den. Follow the string of clues to find out who it was.

*Word clues are strung together so that the last letter of one is beside the first letter of the next, horizontally, vertically, or diagonally. Words are in straight lines, and the number of letters in each is given. Crimes usually start with a **motive**, so let's start there. We've also filled in the first letter of each word for you. This string of clues will lead you to the culprit. Who is it?*

1.(6) MOTIVE

2.(9) F

3.(5) A

4.(5) L

6.(8) E

7.(7) W

8.(5) T

9.(3) L

10.(10) C

```
N O I S S E F N O C
E N A N C Y N G E O
W C Y K R O C I F R
I H N E D L L E O K
T S A E I T V T O Y
N I R A D I R R T N
E R R A T I C I P O
S T G O S O V S R S
S N M H R S O E I R
I Y K L O G I C N A
A G N I B I L A T C
```

Who was it?

51

Nancy wants to give you this message. She says it doesn't require instructions.

She says that you'll be right on top of the code and will follow the letters to make words back and forth, up and down, and all around. We're not so sure about that, but it's her book . . .

START

U	R	L	I	F	E	N	K	S	S
O	R	T	E	N	O	O	I	G	O
Y	I	O	U	F	I	G	L	N	L
G	E	Y	I	E	R	U	L	I	V
N	S	N	T	O	U	T	S	H	I
I	T	E	H	W	U	O	W	T	N
K	O	K	I	L	L	Y	I	U	G
S	I	R	T	U	O	H	T	E	A
E	N	S	Y	O	U	R	S	L	P
P	R	A	H	S	E	L	Z	Z	U

_____

_____

_____.

NANCY DREW

ANSWERS

Page 3

o... f ☐ ü

Page 4

Salad bar

Page 5

To be a normal teenager

Page 6

I think the ability to sleuth is an attractive quality in a woman.

Page 7

We count 28:

ADE	GJK	BAJ	DIE	EJG	BIK
AEB	GKH	BIJ	EIJ	BEG	AJC
BEF	CGK	BKJ	FEJ	AIJ	FJG
AIB	BFG	BGJ	BJC	BGC	BEJ
CGH	AIE	CJK	BKC		

Page 10

Others first

Page 11

Bess: Arson   Ned: Bribery
Nancy Drew: Embezzlement   Trish: Extortion
Corky: Kidnapping   George: Forgery
Inga: Stalking

Puzzle title: Mixed Up in Crime

(Get it? The words "mixed up" are in "crime"!)

Page 12

Page 15
Murderer

Page 16
Tired, Credit, Bored, Fred, Predict, Shred, Redwood, Predator

Page 17

Do you think my mind is a powerful tool?

—George to Bess

Page 18

Undercovers

Page 19

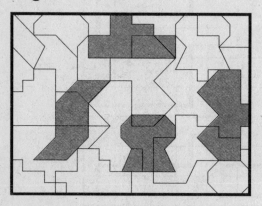

Page 23

Be quiet! Don't wake him up!

Page 24

Case Closed

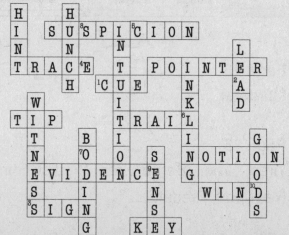

Page 25

Alex — 2

Elliott — 1

Sydonia — 7

Cassie — 4

Zeb — 5

Hudi — 3

CJ — 6

Wayne — 8

Page 26

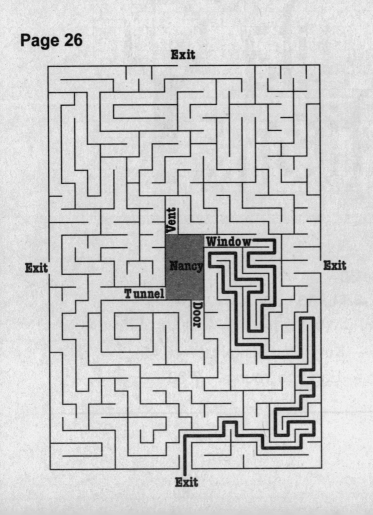

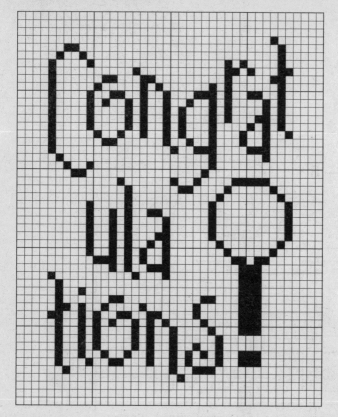

Page 30

Ned — Mu Shoo Pork — 7:00

Corky — Ma Po Tou Foo — 6:30

Inga — Kung Pao Ming Har — 6:45

Trish — Egg Foo Young — 7:30

Page 31
Manners

Page 32
Oh, honey-cheeks. Read the fine print.
No refunds. No exchanges.
                    —Barbara Barbara to Nancy

Page 37
You're a makeover waiting to happen!
                    —Barbara Barbara to Nancy

Page 38

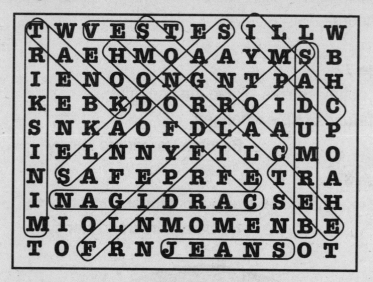

Inga's commentary: Well, we may be on the brink of a penny loafer fashion moment. Or not.

Page 39

Yes. They had dinner today.

Page 40

Where do judges eat lunch?
At the food court!

Page 41

I want to be honest with my father, but I also want to help Jane and her little girl. It's what you call a moral dilemma.

—Nancy Drew to Ned

Page 43

Cafeteria nutrition

Page 44

Will — Freezer
Gems — Fish tank
Painting — Behind a Nancy Drew poster
$$$ — Sunk in a lake
Gold — Trash can

Page 45

Pokey
Cooler
Tank
Clink
Coop

Page 46

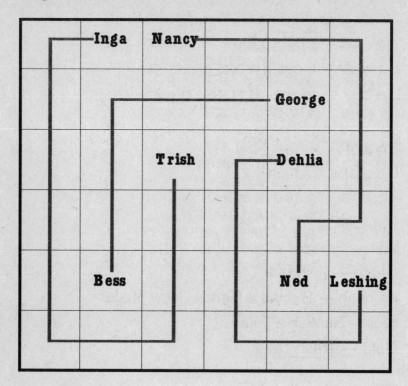

Inga Nancy George Trish Dehlia Bess Ned Leshing

Page 47

A — size 9
B — size 7
C — size 6
D — size 8

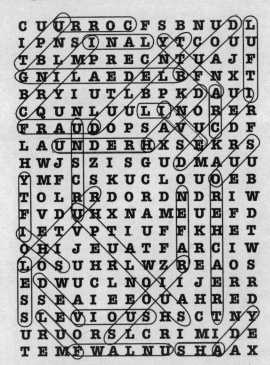

```
C U U R R O C F S B N U D L
I P N S I N A L Y T C O U U
T B L M P R E C N T U A J F
G N I L A E D E L B F N X T
B R Y I U T L B P K D A U I
C Q U N L U U L I N O R E R
F R A U D O P S A V U C D F
L A U N D E R H X S E K R S
H W J S Z I S G U D M A U U
Y M F C S K U C L O U O E B
T O L R R D O R D N D R I W
F V D U H X N A M E U E F D
I E T V P T I U F F K H E T
O H I J E U A T F A R C I W
L O S U H R L W Z R E A O S
E D W U C L N O I J E R R
S S E A I E E O U A H R E D
S L E V I O U S H S C T N Y
U R U O R S L C R I M I D E
T E M F W A L N U S H A A X
```

Page 50

The restaurant owner is lying and might be an accomplice. The robber ran into the restaurant.

Page 51

Motive, footprint, alibi, logic, evidence, witness, trail, lie, confession. It was Nancy! "I'm so sorry!" says Nancy. "I'll clean it up right away!"

Page 52

Solving a puzzle sharpens your sleuthing skills without risking your life. No one tries to kill you when you figure it out.

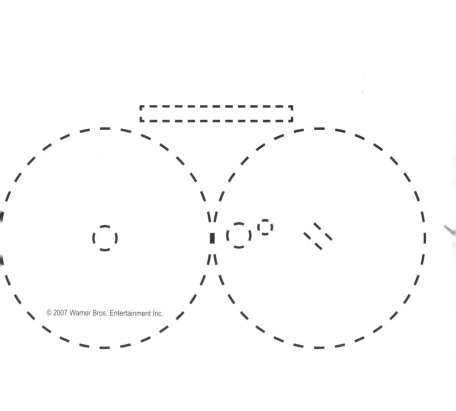

Nancy Drew's Code Breaker Wheel!

Use the wheel to make and break secret codes with your friends.

1. Following the dashed lines, cut out the two wheels and the fastener strip.
2. Cut out the circle on the letter wheel and the two windows on the picture wheel.
3. Cut the two slits on the picture wheel.
4. Insert one side of the fastener into one slit on the picture wheel, then insert the other side of the fastener into the other slit on the picture wheel. Push the fastener down.
5. Insert both ends of the fastener into the hole in the letter wheel with the letter side facing up.
6. Turn your code breaker until the letter you want to decode appears in one window. The other window shows the top secret code!

Nancy Drew's
Code Breaker!

NANCY
DREW

Look for more books about Nancy Drew at your favorite store!

US $5.99 / $6.99 CAN
ISBN-13:   978-1-4169-3380-9
ISBN-10:   1-4169-3380-8

EAN

9 781416 933809

50599

Alvin's
SECRET
CODE

by CLIFFORD B. HICKS

PQE351193